Connect is published by Stone Arch Books
A Capstone Imprint
1710 Roe Crest Drive
North Mankato, Minnesota 56003
www.capstonepub.com

Library of Congress Cataloging-in-Publication Data
Gunderson, Jessica, author.
 Emma's new beginning / by Jessica Gunderson; cover art by Tony Foti.
     pages cm. — (U.S. Immigration in the 1900s)
 Summary: In 1910 eleven-year-old Emma and her ethnically German family immigrate to America from Russia to escape poverty and tyranny, but on her journey she encounters hardships on the overcrowded ship, inspection at Ellis Island, and the struggle to reunite with her father and brother in North Dakota.
  ISBN 978-1-4965-0500-2 (library binding) — ISBN 978-1-4965-0501-9 (pbk.) — ISBN 978-1-4965-2362-4 (ebook pdf)
1. Ellis Island Immigration Station (N.Y. and N.J.)—Juvenile fiction. 2. Immigrant children—United States—Juvenile fiction. 3. Emigration and immigration—Fiction. 4. Russian Germans—Juvenile fiction. 5. Families—Juvenile fiction. 6. North Dakota—Juvenile fiction. [1. Emigration and immigration—Fiction. 2. Immigrants—Fiction. 3. Russian Germans—Fiction. 4. Russian Americans—Fiction. 5. German Americans—Fiction. 6. Family life—Fiction.] I. Foti, Anthony J., illustrator. II. Title.
  PZ7.G963Elm 2015
  [Fic]—dc23   2015001898

Designer: Veronica Scott
Cover Illustration: Tony Foti

Printed in China.
03302015   008868RRDF15

Emma's
New Beginning

By Jessica Gunderson

stone arch
books

Chapter 1
A New Beginning

1910

My father's voice rings loud and clear in the tiny room. "We are going to America!" he booms, smiling.

I do not smile. I hold my breath to keep in my sobs. My ribs feel like they're going to crack into a million pieces. I cannot imagine leaving home. I cannot imagine journeying over the ocean to a place so far away.

My little brother, Karl, pipes up. "Where is America? Is it far away?"

Father nods and grins down at Karl. "Yes. It will take

many days to get there. We will travel on a big ship! It will be a great adventure!"

Karl's eyes gleam in excitement.

"Can I bring Zizzy?" my little sister, Helene, asks. Zizzy is a small wooden horse that she carries everywhere.

Father grins at her. "Of course!"

I glance at my older sister, Katarina. She is staring stone-faced at Father. Finally she blurts out, "I don't want to leave Russia."

Katarina and I rarely agree. We don't have anything in common. But this time, she's taken the words right out of my mouth.

Father's smile drops. He looks at me. "What do you think, Emma?"

I am surprised. As the middle child, I'm often overlooked, caught between my older siblings, Gustav and Katarina, and my younger siblings, Karl and Helene. Overlooked until someone needs me, that is. And now, Father needs me to side with him, to join his enthusiasm.

"I don't want to leave Russia either," I tell him. "Odessa is my home."

Katarina flashes me a sideways look. She's surprised I agreed with her. Sometimes we disagree just to disagree, even if deep inside we really do agree. But this is different. This time I had to speak up.

"No, Emma," Father says. "Odessa is not your home. We are a people without a home."

Katarina and I look at him, surprised. Even Karl and Helene quiet their excited murmurs. "That's not true!" Katarina argues. "We've always lived here. How can Russia not be our home?"

We listen as Father explains the history of our German people. Over a hundred years ago, in the late 1700s, our ancestors left Germany to settle in a German colony in Ukraine, part of the Russian Empire. The Russian czar, Catherine the Great, promised our people we could keep our language and customs. And we would never have to fight in the Russian Army.

But one hundred years later, the Russian czar broke Catherine's promise and placed new rules on us. We had to go to Russian schools and were forbidden to speak German in public. Our men and boys had to serve in the Russian Army. Our people are poor, and it seems we never have enough to eat.

Still, I think, *even though we are poor, we are happy. Aren't we?*

As though Father can read my mind, he says, "We will be happier in America. We will have enough food to eat. We will be free to practice our language and customs. And Gustav won't be forced to serve in the army."

"But what about my friends?" Katarina says. Her voice breaks into a sob, and tears spill from her eyes. Without waiting for an answer, she runs from the room. Katarina is thirteen, but she cries more than five-year-old Helene. Usually I am annoyed by Katarina's constant angry crying, but today I wish I could cry, too.

"What will we do there?" I ask.

"Your Uncle Elmer has a farm in a place called North Dakota. I know you have never met him, but he has invited me to farm with him," Father says.

Karl grabs Helene's hands and spins her around the room. "We're going to America!" he shouts. The children dance wildly until they collapse into a pile of giggles. I watch them in somber silence until Father stands and puts a hand on my shoulder. "America will be a new beginning for us," he says.

Chapter 2
Train to the Unknown

The shrill train whistle pierces the air. Black smoke rises from the smokestack as the train chugs toward the station. With one hand I clutch Helene's tiny palm. With the other, I grip my suitcase. The case holds the only belongings I can take to America. I try not to think about everything I had to leave behind, but the images swim before my eyes. A cuckoo clock, made especially for me by my grandfather. A life-sized baby doll named Inga that I have had since I was younger than Helene. My favorite boots. Three dresses. A hat with feathers that I never wore but loved anyway.

The only time I shed tears was when I gave Inga to a neighbor child. Helene tried to comfort me. "You can get a new doll in America!" she said.

"I'm eleven," I told her. "I'm too old for baby dolls."

Before I gave Inga away, I took off her dress and folded it into my suitcase. The dress, made of blue-and-white gingham, was the last thing my mother gave to me before she died. Even though I am too old for dolls, I will keep that dress for the rest of my life.

The train blasts into the station, and Helene clutches my skirts, frightened by the noise and the gigantic, looming train cars. Karl races along the platform until Father scolds him. Katarina stares sullenly at her boots, and Gustav stares straight ahead. We've never been on a train. We've never even left Odessa.

A sudden fear grips me. What if the train crashes? What if the boat sinks? What if America sends us back?

But I don't have time to be scared. The conductor orders us to the very last passenger car. I grip Helene's hand more tightly as the crowd on the platform surges toward the train. Bodies bump against me, and tall heads block my view. Where is Father? Panic strangles my throat. What if I have lost him in this crowd?

"Father?" I call. "Father!"

But my words are lost in the hissing of the train and the shouts of the crowd.

"Zizzy!" I hear Helene cry. She wrenches free from my grip and scuttles into the crowd.

"Helene!" I scream. I turn to shove backward through the sea of passengers, but the bodies are too tightly packed. Everyone is pushing forward, and no one is paying attention to me. I'm just one young girl among so many others.

My vision blurs with tears. I have lost my little sister. I have lost Father. I am alone.

A hand tugs my arm. I turn to see a dark-haired girl about my age. She pulls me backward, and we tumble out of the crowd. I see Helene, standing on the platform, clutching her wooden horse. Tears stream down her cheeks. I rush toward her and gather her in my arms. "I dropped Zizzy," Helene wails. "And then I was all alone!"

"It's okay," I tell her. "I'm here now."

The train whistle shrills. "We have to board the train," I tell Helene, tugging her behind me toward the passenger car. I scan the crowd for the dark-haired girl, but I don't see her.

As we near the car door, I see my father leaning out, looking worriedly over the crowd of people. "Step back, sir!" the car attendant orders.

"Father! We're here!" I call. I push through the people and hoist Helene into my father's arms. Then I step up into the train, just as the final boarding call sounds. I take one last breath of Russian air before the door closes and the train lurches forward into the unknown.

Chapter 3
A New Friend

The train car is packed so tightly we can barely move. Only the elderly have places to sit. The rest of us have to stand. I try to keep my balance as the train sways left and right. The knots in my stomach twist and untwist. I think I might throw up. But at least we are all here — Father, Helene, Karl, Katarina . . .

"Where's Gustav?" I gasp, searching the faces for my older brother.

Father shrugs and smiles. "He went wandering through the train," he says.

I nod and relax. Gustav, nearly seventeen, is often

disappearing. He doesn't have much patience for us younger siblings.

Karl fidgets, craning his neck to look around. "I can't see anything," he whines. "How long until we get to the ship?"

"A long time," Father tells him. "First we go to Poland. And then to Germany. Then we board the ship."

I sigh. The train journey will be long. And there's nothing to do but stand here.

I close my eyes and try to remember everything I can about Odessa, for I know I will never see the city again. I see our tiny home. I see the walls around our German settlement, separating us from the rest of the city. I see the Potemkin Stairs, two hundred steps that rise from the seashore into the city. I remember teaching Helene to walk up those steps when she was a toddler. I can still see the proud joy on her face after she climbed each step. Helene will probably never remember Odessa. I have to hold onto the memories for her.

Soon I get used to the swaying of the train, and it nearly lulls me to sleep on my feet. Each time the train stops at a station, passengers get off. Finally seats open up, and I fall into one, pulling Helene onto my lap.

In the seat in front of me, I see the dark-haired girl who found Helene. When she catches me staring at her, she blushes and looks down. I lean forward. "Thank you for finding my sister," I tell her.

The girl shrugs. "It was no trouble," she says, her voice soft and shy.

"I'm Emma," I tell her.

"My name is Ruth."

"I'm Helene!" my little sister cries. "We're going to America!"

Ruth grins at her and seems to relax. "I am too," she says.

"Are you all alone?" I ask her.

She nods. "My father is already in America. He will meet me when I get off the boat."

As she speaks, I realize she is Jewish. I've never spoken to a Jew before. The Jews in Odessa were always separate, just as we Germans were.

Just then, Katarina looms over me. "You shouldn't be

talking to her," she hisses. She yanks Helene from my lap and drags her to another seat.

I turn to apologize to Ruth, but she won't meet my eyes. "She's right," Ruth murmurs. "You shouldn't be talking to me. Everyone looks down on us because we're Jewish."

"Not everyone," I tell her. "Not me."

I climb over the seat and plop down next to Ruth. I flash a smile at her surprised face and say, "Tell me about you. Tell me your story."

Chapter 4
Paradise

"Five years ago," Ruth begins, "two of my uncles were killed in the pogrom. Do you know what that is?"

I shake my head.

"Pogroms are when anti-Jewish people attack us, rob our stores, and invade our homes," she explains. "I was only five years old, but I remember being so scared. Hiding under the bed, afraid of every sound. I remember my father carrying my uncles' dead bodies into our home, one right after the other. I remember the Shiva for both of them."

At my confused look, Ruth adds, "Shiva is seven days of mourning."

I nod, and Ruth goes on, "Ever since then, my father saved every cent to immigrate to America. He went over with my aunt and cousins last year. He finally saved enough to send me, too. My mother will come later with my little siblings."

I can't imagine making the journey alone. At least I have my family around me!

"My father says we will be welcome in America," Ruth goes on. "We won't be spit on or called names because we're Jewish. It sounds like paradise!"

"I have been called names, too, because I'm German," I tell her. "I remember once, when I was only seven years old, a group of older boys surrounded me and taunted me." I shudder. "I thought they were going to kill me!"

"America will be different," Ruth says. "We can be free to be ourselves, whether Jewish or German."

My stomach rumbles with hunger. "And we will have food to eat!" I say with a laugh.

Ruth and I talk for hours. We discover we will be on

the same ship to America. When darkness settles over the train, Ruth drifts off to sleep, but I am wide awake. I can't stop thinking about what America will be like. Will it really be like paradise, as Ruth says?

Chapter 5
Steerage

The ship rises from the sea like a monster, casting shadows over the harbor and blocking the sun. I've never felt so terrified in my life.

Helene cries and stuffs her face into my skirt. I pat her back, trying to calm my fear. Even Karl, usually so excited, stares at up at the enormous ship, his eyes wide and his lips trembling.

Father shoots a stern glare in our direction. "Come on, children. Time to board the ship."

"It's . . . it's so big!" I say.

"Would you rather take a tiny boat across the ocean?" Father demands.

I shake my head and scan the docks for Ruth. I don't see her anywhere. Katarina catches me looking and glares. She knows I'm looking for Ruth, and she doesn't approve.

I follow my father toward the ship, gripping Helene's hand tightly as we weave through the crowds. I won't let her disappear this time. And I won't let Father out of my sight.

As we stand in line to board the ship, I hear all sorts of languages — Russian, German, Yiddish, and others I've never heard before. *Are we all going to America?* I wonder. How will we ever be able to understand each other?

Fear rises in my throat as I realize I don't know much English. I know yes and no. And cat, dog, and horse. Father has said it doesn't matter. Where we are going, most people will speak German and Russian. I can learn English slowly. But what if I am separated from my family? How will I manage?

Helene looks up and sees the tears watering in my eyes. I blink them away and smile down at her. I point to Zizzy, clutched in her hand. "Horse," I say in English.

We are stuffed like sausages in third-class, or steerage. *Steerage*. The word makes us sound like animals. My stomach roils from the odor of so many bodies so close together. Rows of bunks line the walls. And it's dark. No windows.

We lay our belongings onto bunks. I feel dizzy, even though the ship hasn't embarked yet. Maybe some fresh air will help. I call to Karl and Helene, and they follow me through the ship. I pay close attention so we don't get lost. On the way, we pass a large, noisy cafeteria. I lean in and spot Ruth, sitting quietly. Her face widens with joy when she sees me, and she rushes toward me. I want to hug her, but I feel suddenly shy.

"We're going to the upper deck," I tell her.

She agrees to come with us. We climb one stairwell after another. Ruth gestures to the locked gates that keep us from the first-class and second-class cabins. "Look at that!" she says. "We're fenced in."

"Like animals," I add.

We finally reach the deck, where we join other passengers on the railing. The ship blasts its horn. I clutch the railing as the ship moves away from the harbor, launching us across the sea to our new lives.

Chapter 6
Seasick

I am sick. So are Katarina and Gustav. I lie on my bunk, my stomach churning with each lurch of the ship. I sleep miserably, never knowing if it's day or night. Sometimes when I wake, I see Helene's scared eyes peering down at me. Other times, I wake to find Ruth spooning water into my mouth.

After two whole days of tossing feverishly, I can finally stomach the food Father brings me from the cafeteria, even though it tastes horrible. I look around for Katarina and Gustav, but they are no longer in their bunks.

"Katarina is in the infirmary," Father explains. At my horrified look, he adds, "She's okay. But she developed a cough along with seasickness. I had to send her to the sickroom so she didn't infect others."

I nod. I don't get along with Katarina, but I hope she's okay. "And Gustav?" I ask.

Father shrugs. "Gustav is . . . ?"

"Always wandering off?" I finish.

Father smiles. "You know our family well, Emma. You are the middle child, the heart of this family. I don't know what I'd do without you."

I smile back at him, but for some reason his words make me feel sad.

"There was a girl here, caring for me," I tell Father.

His eyes darken, and he looks away. "The Jew girl?" he says. "You shouldn't be rubbing elbows with Jews. They're not like us."

"And we're not like them!" I say. "Why does it matter?"

Father has no answer. We are silent for a few minutes, and then I say, "Father, we are going to America, where everyone is equal and no one is looked down upon. In America, we will start anew. Shouldn't we get rid of our old ideas about Jews?"

Before Father can answer, Helene and Karl rush into the cabin and fling themselves onto my bed. Father stands and pats my head. "I hope America is everything you dreamed," he says.

The ship sways, and my tender stomach coils. "I just want to get off this ship," I say with a moan.

Chapter 7

Discovery

I get out of bed and decide to find Ruth. I step slowly through the crowded cabin. Children are shrieking and crying. Laughter booms from some of the men. Women hold their children or speak to each other urgently in unfamiliar languages. Some sit silently, miserable.

I remember my earlier conversation with Father. We are all humans with the same goal — to go to America. We all want to begin a new life. Why should we despise one another?

I make my way toward the cafeteria. But soon I'm lost. I turn down a dark hallway, then another. I hear nothing but the roar of steam engines. My heart flutters, and I quicken my step. Then, up ahead, I hear loud laughter. I rush toward the sound.

Clouds of cigar smoke tumble from an open doorway. I hold back a cough and peer in. Men are crowded around tables, puffing on pipes, holding tall mugs, and tossing playing cards between them. In the corner, a group of young men sing a rowdy song.

I am just about to turn and run when I see a familiar face. Gustav. He clutches a hand of cards, peering intently. The other men at his table stare at him. He finally tosses a card onto the table. The man across from him grins and throws down his whole hand. Then, to my horror, I watch Gustav drop several coins into the man's hand.

Gambling! Gustav is gambling. My mind races. Gambling is forbidden in our church. So is drinking and smoking. Father will kill him! Where did he get the money? Did he steal from Father?

A hand clamps down on my shoulder. I scream, but the sound evaporates in the din of noise.

I turn to see a young man with bushy, dark eyebrows glaring down at me. He shouts something into my ear. I can't understand him and only shake in fear.

He points to my skirt, then shakes his head and swipes his forefinger into a big X. I stare, confused, as he repeats the motion. Finally I understand. No girls allowed. Men only.

I take one more glance at Gustav. He slams his cards down and stands, moving toward the doorway. I lift my skirt and run as fast as I can down the long hallway.

I don't know what to do. Should I tell Father? Should I confront Gustav?

I find my way back to the stairwell leading to the deck. I no longer want to find Ruth. Instead, I feel like being alone.

Rain slaps my face as I stand at the railing, looking out at the vicious waves crashing in the sea. No land is in sight. We are a lonely ship of passengers. Will America be a safe harbor for us?

I hear someone clanking along the slippery deck. I turn to see Gustav, his face dripping with rain. "Is that you, little Emma?" he says, squinting. He stands next to me at the railing and looks toward the sea. "Have you spotted her yet?"

"Have I spotted who?"

He grins. "The woman who stands in New York harbor, welcoming the immigrants. 'Give me your tired, your poor . . .'"

"The Statue of Liberty!" I say.

He nudges me. "Let's try to be the first to spot her, okay?"

"We'll have to stand out here for days," I say. "We're not even close to New York!"

We stand and watch the horizon in silence. I make a decision. I won't tell Father. Maybe Gustav has learned his lesson.

Chapter 8
First Glimpse

For the next ten days at sea, Ruth and I spend time together every chance we get. On calm, sunny days, we sit on deck. Sometimes a boy plays a harmonica, and we all dance. I watch a young Hungarian man dance with a Polish girl. They can't understand each other, but they dance anyway. First-class and second-class passengers on the decks above look down at us. Once in a while, they throw down an apple or a piece of candy. I can't stand the pity in their eyes.

Still I love the days on deck, because staying below in steerage is horrible. People are sick and scratching from lice. The food is awful. There aren't enough tables for everyone, and the children have to eat on the floor.

Karl and Helene spend much of their time with the Schweitzer children, who are also Germans from Odessa. Their mother, Mrs. Schweitzer, is kindly and looks after Karl and Helene as if they are her own. She tells me her husband went to America two years ago to work at a factory in Chicago. He finally saved up enough money to send for them. "I hope I recognize him," Mrs. Schweitzer says with a laugh. "It has been so long!"

After a few days, Katarina is released from the sick room, but she still doesn't look well. When she is below deck, she hides her cough. But sometimes out on deck, I see her coughing loudly into the wind. I am scared. For her and for us. What if she dies? Or what if she is so sick they don't let her into America?

At night, I pray to God. I pray for Gustav and Katarina. And Father and my two little siblings. I even pray for Ruth. Ruth says that the Jewish God and the Christian God are the same, so I know He is looking out for her, too.

Gustav disappears a lot, and I tell myself that he is just wandering the ship, not gambling with Father's money. I often stand at the railing, scanning the horizon for the Statue of Liberty. But Gustav rarely joins me.

⸺᷽⸺

"There she is!" someone shouts.

The deck is crowded with people hoping to catch their first glimpse of America. I crane my neck and spot the top of Lady Liberty's torch. Tears burn my eyes. Tears of joy. And tears of sadness, for I will have to say goodbye to Ruth. She will stay in New York. And I will go to North Dakota, far away from New York City.

"I wanna see the statue!" Helene cries.

I lift her onto my shoulders. Lady Liberty looms closer, and behind her, tall buildings rise. Taller buildings than I've ever seen.

Next to me, Ruth tugs my arm. "Soon we'll have to board the ferry to Ellis Island," she says. "And say goodbye."

I lower Helene to the floor and pull a scrap of paper from my skirt pocket. On it I've written the address of my uncle in North Dakota. I hand it to Ruth. "Will you write to me?"

Ruth smiles. "The first chance I get!"

We hug goodbye. "This is the beginning, not the end," I tell her.

Chapter 9
Ellis Island

We are herded from the ship to a ferry that takes us to Ellis Island. When I step off the boat onto the island, a thrill passes from my feet all the way to my heart. I am in America! I am an American now.

Guards shout orders in different languages. I cling to Helene and Karl, praying I won't lose them in the confusion. A guard roughly grabs my coat and pins a number onto my collar and then motions me toward the enormous red-brick building. I follow my father as we climb the stairs into the largest room I've ever seen. The

sun's rays shine through tall windows. "Get in the line!"
a guard shouts to us in German.

We shuffle through in line for what seems like hours.
Helene and Karl whimper from exhaustion, and Katarina
looks pale and weak as she leans against the low iron
railing that separates the lines of people. Gustav and
Father stare straight ahead.

As we climb the stairs that lead into the Registry
Room, I notice a tall man in a military uniform standing
at the top of the steps, staring at each immigrant who
passes. Once in a while he pulls someone from the line
and shouts something I can't make out. "He's watching
us for something," I murmur to Katarina. "Act normal
and don't cough."

Katarina stiffens as we pass the uniformed man. As
his eyes graze over her, I see her shoulders tense with
effort not to cough.

When the man's gaze finally lifts and moves to
Gustav, I let out a sigh of relief. Katarina passed!

Next we come to a man who holds a thin metal
stick in his hand. He examines each immigrant's eyes,

pulling up their eyelid with the stick. I look worriedly at Katerina. *Please don't cough,* I think.

The medical inspector peers at Katarina's eyes, then lets her pass. Karl steps forward and lifts his face for the examination.

I am so relieved by Katarina's passing that Karl's shriek startles me. "No!" he cries. "No!"

The inspector shouts at him in English, pushing Karl from the line. Karl tries to wrench free, but the inspector shoves him away. Karl turns to me, his wide eyes scared. I see the inspector has written a large *CT* across his coat.

"They're sending me back, Emma. They're making me go back to Russia!" Karl screams at me.

"Everything will be okay," I tell him, trying to remain calm. I stare numbly as Karl is led away from the inspection line. Will they send him back to Russia? Karl is too little to survive on his own. *This can't be happening,* I think. *What if I never see my little brother again?*

The inspector shouts at me. It's my turn. I try to hold still as he pries the metal piece under my eyelid and lifts up. He nods and motions me forward. "My brother," I say to him, gesturing in the direction Karl went. "I need to be with him!"

The doctor shakes his head at me. He says something in English, but I don't understand.

"You're holding up the line!" someone behind me shouts in German.

I move forward and clutch Katarina's shoulder. "We have to tell Father they've taken Karl!" Tears bubble in my eyes.

Katarina cranes her neck to look back at me. I expect to see tears in her eyes, too, but all I see is hardness. "How do you like your America now?" she snaps. "Some paradise!"

Chapter 10
Worry

Father drops his head into his hands. "Not Karl," he moans.

"I will stay and wait for him, Father," I offer. "You and the others go on to America."

"No," he says. "We will all wait."

Father speaks rapidly to a German interpreter. As he speaks, I watch the immigration officials interview immigrants in the nearby line. Some pass through. Others are detained for various reasons. No job skills. No male relative. Not old enough to enter without an adult. Likely to become a public nuisance. I have to look away. I can't bear the wretched disappointment on their faces.

I wonder about Ruth. Has her father come to fetch her? What if he doesn't show up? Will she be sent back to Russia?

Father returns, looking dejected. "We have to go through the immigration line. Then we will wait for Karl."

We crowd into a corral marked with a *B*.

At last we reach the immigration officer at the end of the line. He stares at Father intently. "Name?" he barks in German.

"Friedrich Gustav Weiss," Father answers.

"Occupation?"

"Machinist."

"Who do you know in America?"

"My brother."

"How much money do you have?"

Father reaches into his pocket. His eyes widen. "I had money," he stammers. "It was right here!" He stuffs his hand into another pocket, then another. No money.

My heart launches into my throat. Without money, we will be sent back.

I look at Gustav. His face is pale. He reaches into his pocket and pulls out a handful of coins. "Father!" he cries. "I have your money."

Father frowns in confusion. "You dropped it," Gustav says. His face is now bright red. He's lying, I know. He stole Father's money to gamble.

Father snatches the money and shows it to the official. The official nods. "Next!" he says.

"How could you?" I snap at Gustav.

Gustav pretends he doesn't hear me, but I know he heard every word. Loud and clear.

We shuffle into another large room, where we will wait for word about Karl. Women and children huddle together in corners. Men pace back and forth. Everyone has the same look in their eyes. Worry.

I wonder how many will be sent back. And I wonder, will we?

For hours we wait. Helene is scared, and I try to comfort her by reciting her favorite fairy tales. But she stops me halfway through one tale. "Emma," she whispers, looking up at the tall ceiling. "Is this where we will live now?"

"No," I tell her. "We are just here for a little while. Don't worry."

Just then, an official steps into the room and shouts my father's name. Father rushes toward him, then they both disappear through another door. After an eternity, he reappears. This time with Karl.

I leap to my feet. Karl grins and skips toward us. "I don't have trachoma! My eyes are healthy!" he shouts. "And I got a piece of candy!"

We all give Karl a big hug. Even Katarina is smiling.

Finally, I think, *our new life can begin.*

Chapter 11
Sacrifice

New York City is noisy and lively. Horses clop down the streets. Even a few automobiles whiz by. Vendors call to us to buy their goods. People of all different colors saunter past. Tall brick buildings cast shadows on the sidewalk. We are here. This is America.

We make our way to the train station and board a train bound for Chicago. This train is not as crowded as the one in Russia. I fall into a deep sleep as the train pulls out of the station. When I wake, the sun is shining. Wide expanses of fields flash by in the windows. I look around for Karl and Helene, and I spot the Schweitzers, our friends from the boat, toward the back of the train car. I smile at Mrs. Schweitzer, happy to see a familiar face in such unfamiliar surroundings.

I sit back and watch America spin past. I am amazed at all the wooden buildings — houses, barns, stores. In Russia most buildings were made of stone. I close my eyes and wonder what our new home will be like.

Will it be made of wood? Brightly painted? Will I still share a room with my sisters? What will life on a farm be like? I have only known city life. Will it snow in the winter? I have never seen snow before, although I have seen it in pictures.

"Wake up, Emma!" Father shakes my shoulder. "We are in Chicago."

I step from the train, rubbing my eyes. I see Mrs. Schweitzer hug a dark-haired man. The children clamor about him. He must be Mr. Schweitzer.

Where is Gustav? I wonder. And then I see him coming toward us. His lips are trembling, as though he's about to cry. I've never seen Gustav cry. Fear clenches my stomach. What has happened?

"Father," Gustav says. "I have to tell you . . ." His eyes flit away, and he can't look my father in the face. "I lost our money."

"Lost?" Father thunders. "What do you mean, lost?"

"I . . . there was a card game," Gustav stammers. "On the train. These men . . . I thought I could beat them. I won so many games on the ship. I thought . . . I thought I could make more money."

"You gambled away our money?" Father says. He's no longer shouting. His voice is even and angered. "That money was for our train tickets to North Dakota." He glares at Gustav. Then his glare collapses into sorrow. "What will we do?" he whispers.

I turn away. My whole body is shaking. I know this is my fault. If only I'd told Father about Gustav gambling on the ship. Father could've stopped him. But now it is too late. Our money is gone.

My thoughts echo Father's words. *What will we do?*

Mrs. Schweitzer steps toward Father, smiling. "This is where we say goodbye," she says. Her smile falls when she sees the look on his face.

As he tells her what has happened, she nods. "How much do you need?" she asks.

"Five dollars for each ticket," Father says.

Mrs. Schweitzer turns to her husband and whispers to him. I feel a glimmer of hope. Perhaps the Schweitzers will loan us money.

But my hopes are squashed when Mr. Schweitzer shakes his head sadly. "I cannot help you," he tells Father. "I spent my last dollars on the train fare for my family."

In that moment, I want to murder Gustav. But Gustav looks so sad and guilty I can't help but feel sorry for him. I know he didn't mean to lose the money. He didn't mean to put us in this horrible situation.

The walls of the station seem to close in around me. I rush up the steps and step out onto the sidewalk. A cold wind batters against my thin coat, and I shiver and look up at the tall buildings. The sun is buried behind clouds. Chicago seems so dark and forbidding. How will we survive here with no money and nowhere to go?

I notice that a man on the corner is watching me.

I turn to go back into the station, but the man strides toward me and grabs my shoulder. I can't move. He grins down at me, teeth crooked and eyes dark. He says something I don't understand. "No!" I say in English. "No!"

He smiles again, more kindly this time, and points to my earrings. Then he pulls out a handful of coins.

He wants to buy my earrings.

I touch my earrings. They were a gift from my grandmother. Pure gold and diamonds, worth more than just a few coins. But maybe . . .

"More!" I say to the man.

He frowns and pulls out paper money. "Five?" he says.

The tickets are five dollars each, Father said. I pull out one earring, snatch the five dollars, and drop the earring into the man's hand. Then I touch the other earring. "Five!" I say.

The man sighs and mutters to himself. Then he pulls out another five dollars.

I drop the other earring into the man's hand, grab

the money, and run back into the station. I have enough money for two tickets. But only two. Who will go? And who will stay?

Chapter 12
A Place to Stay

Father stares at the money, then back at me. "You sold your earrings?"

I shrug as though parting with the earrings doesn't bother me. Gustav won't look me in the eye. He stares at the ground, his shoulders in a miserable slump.

"We have to get to North Dakota somehow," I tell him.

Father shakes his head. "No. When we go, we'll go together."

"But what about the spring planting?" Katarina asks. "You said Uncle Elmer needed you. I will go with you.

I can tend the house while you work in the fields." She smiles triumphantly at me, as though she's won a game. I know she'd be glad to be rid of us, at least for a while.

"You are right about the spring planting," Father says. "But I need to take Gustav."

"Gustav!" Katarina gasps. "But he's the one who —"

"Lost the money," Gustav interrupts. "I won't go."

Just then, Mrs. Schweitzer speaks up. "I can take the little ones," she says. "But we don't have room for more."

Terror seizes me at the thought of being separated from Helene and Karl. I want to snatch the money from Father's hand and say, *Never mind.*

Mrs. Schweitzer sees my stricken face and gazes thoughtfully from me to Katarina. "Unless you can earn your keep," she says.

"I'll do anything!" I say, just as Katarina says, more suspiciously, "What do you want us to do?"

Mr. Schweitzer clears his throat. "The older one could work in the factory as a seamstress," he tells Mrs. Schweitzer. He seems too nervous to speak to us directly. "But the middle girl might be too young."

Father considers the idea, then shoos us away to speak privately to the Schweitzers.

"Factory!" Katarina hisses under her breath. "I might as well go back to Russia."

"Hush!" I mutter to her. "The Schweitzers are being kind."

Katarina grunts. "Yeah, and they'll make money off us at the same time," she says. "Apparently in America, kindness isn't free."

Father returns to us, his face pained. "It's settled," he says. "Gustav and I will go to North Dakota. The rest of you will stay with the Schweitzers until we've saved enough money for your train fare."

"How much do we have to pay them?" Katarina asks.

Father's eyes flick away. From the look on his face, I realize the Schweitzers must be charging more than necessary.

I glance at Mrs. Schweitzer, and she flashes me a friendly smile. *Is she really trying to take advantage of us?* I wonder. It's hard to believe. She was so nice on the ship.

Father's words flash into my mind: I hope America is everything you dreamed. I think back over the last few days — Karl's detainment at Ellis Island, Gustav's gambling, selling my earrings for only a fraction of their worth. America has been nothing like I imagined. Not even close.

I square my shoulders. Hopefully the worst is now behind us.

Chapter 13
Chicago

The train rumbles out of sight, carrying Father and Gustav far away to the Great Plains.

"When will we see them again?" Helene asks. Surprisingly, she has no tears in her eyes. The last few days have hardened her to the world.

"Soon," I tell her, though I'm not sure I believe my own words. It could be months, maybe even a year. Maybe never.

"Now we will ride another train," Mr. Schweitzer tells us. "A train in the sky!"

We climb rickety steps that lead to train tracks

propped above the streets. The younger children are excited, but I feel afraid. I have never seen train tracks suspended in air. What if the train falls off the track? And as the train lurches into motion, my fear grows. The cars wobble, and the wheels squeal around curves. I close my eyes, trying not to picture the train toppling to the street below. Then Mrs. Schweitzer tugs my arm. "This is our stop."

We climb down to the sidewalk below. Rickety buildings line the streets, and I catch whiffs of something awful. I say nothing, in order to be polite, but Katarina speaks up. "What is that horrible stench?"

At first Mr. Schweitzer says nothing. Perhaps he didn't hear her, or perhaps he's still nervous around us. Finally he says, "That's the Union Stockyards. Where I work."

"You slaughter animals?" Katarina gasps.

"Katarina!" Mrs. Schweitzer barks. "You will respect your elders."

Katarina glares at Mrs. Schweitzer and then lowers her eyes. "Yes, ma'am," she says. Ever since our mother died, Katarina has been the female in charge. I don't think she's going to like living with Mrs. Schweitzer.

The Schweitzer apartment is tiny — just two rooms and a small kitchen. Mr. Schweitzer looks apologetically at Mrs. Schweitzer, who stands in the doorway, dismayed. I try to hide my own surprise. Mr. Schweitzer has been in America for two years, and this is all he has? Where are the streets paved with gold? America is nothing like any of us imagined.

Still, the apartment is clean, and the children don't seem to mind sleeping piled nearly on top of one another. Katarina and I make do, sleeping stuffed alongside the younger children on a mattress on the floor.

The next morning Katarina goes to the shirt factory to look for work. "The sooner I work, the sooner we'll be out of here," she tells me.

She doesn't come back until dark. As we eat around the small kitchen table, I notice she keeps rubbing her hands and neck. "I'll get used to it," she snaps when she catches me looking at her.

We do get used to it. We get used to everything — the

noise of the elevated train, the stench of the stockyards, the strange languages around us.

Every morning, Katarina and Mr. Schweitzer rise at daybreak to go to work and don't return until late evening. I help Mrs. Schweitzer with the children. No one mentions school.

We get letters from Father, telling us about the farm. "The prairie stretches all the way to the horizon. Not a hill in sight!" he writes. I try to imagine what the prairie looks like.

Katarina comes home one night with her first pay from the factory. She holds out the money to Mrs. Schweitzer. "How much do I owe you for letting us stay here?" she asks in an emotionless voice.

Mrs. Schweitzer takes the money and counts. She shakes her head and looks at Katarina, sadness in her eyes.

"This is barely enough to feed three of you, let alone four," she says.

"So you are taking all of it?" Katarina says.

Mrs. Schweitzer nods.

I expect Katarina to argue, but she doesn't.

That night, I wake to hear Katarina sniffling. I see her crouched in the corner, her head in her hands.

"What's wrong?" I whisper.

She is silent so long I don't think she'll answer. Then her words come out in a rush. "I hate the factory," she says. "The other girls call me names. Hardly anyone speaks German. And we can't talk anyway, or we will get rapped on the hands with a stick. And after days and days of working, I barely made enough to give the Schweitzers." She looks at me, her tears glittering in the moonlight streaming in the window. "How will I ever save enough to get to North Dakota?"

I don't know what to say. I hug her around the shoulders. She seems so small. Even though she's older than me, she seems too young to work in a factory all day. She's barely thirteen.

"Some workers are talking about going on strike," Katarina goes on.

"What is that?" I ask.

"It's when the workers refuse to work until they are

given higher pay and get better working conditions," she explains.

"Does it work?" I ask.

She shrugs. "Sometimes. But I can't imagine the factory ever paying us more. Plus, if I go on strike, I won't get paid at all. I can't afford to lose any wages."

"I know, but . . ."

She shakes her head. "I'm so tired, Emma," she says.

Katarina falls asleep quickly but I lie awake, thinking. I know I am too young to work in the factory. But I'm almost eleven. Surely there is some work I can do. *Tomorrow I'll find something*, I tell myself.

Chapter 14
A New Opportunity

I tell the Schweitzers that I want to find a job. Mrs. Schweitzer does not look happy. "But I need you to help with the children," she says.

"I can pay you to look after Helene and Karl," I tell her.

"I might know of something she can do," Mr. Schweitzer tells his wife.

Mrs. Schweitzer sighs. "I suppose I can make do without you," she says.

A few days later, Mr. Schweitzer tells me that his boss's elderly mother needs someone to clean her home and fix her meals. "She wants an Irish girl, but she's willing to see if you can do the job."

"But I don't know much English," I say. I've picked up a few words from the other children in the neighborhood, but I know it's not enough to communicate with an elderly lady.

Mr. Schweitzer hands me a slip of paper with a name, Kathleen O'Reilly, and an address. "Go to see her tomorrow. She'll decide if you are a good fit. But don't get your hopes up," he adds.

﹌﹏

The next morning, I set off for Mrs. O'Reilly's house. Kathleen O'Reilly. I'm not sure I can pronounce her name correctly, and I repeat it under my breath as I make my way through the Chicago streets.

As I walk, the streets widen and the crowded, run-down brick buildings turn to sturdy, well-kept homes. I reach the address and gaze at the house. *Mrs. O'Reilly must be rich*, I think. Her lawn is sparkling green, and the red bricks seem to glow in the sun. An upstairs window is open, and lace curtains billow in the breeze. I can't believe she lives in this big house all by herself.

I swing open the gate and climb the steps to the front door. My heart hammers as I reach to ring the doorbell. Just as the bell chimes, I realize my mistake. I shouldn't have gone to the front door. I should've gone to the back, where servants would enter.

But it's too late. The door opens a crack, and a voice rings out. "Who is it?"

"Hello," I say in my practiced English. "Mrs. O'Reilly?"

The door opens wider, and a wrinkled face peers through. "I think that's me," she says. "But it's pronounced *RILE - EE*. Not *REEL - EE*."

I nod. I wish I could explain. I want to say sorry for coming to the front door. And sorry for not pronouncing her name correctly. But the English words won't come. All I can say is, "My name is Emma Weiss. Here to clean."

She frowns. "I told him I wanted an Irish girl," she mutters. "You are what?"

"I am Emma —" I begin, but she cuts me off.

"No. What country?"

I want to turn and run. She probably won't let me inside anyway. But then I remember Katarina's exhausted tears. I swallow my fear and say, "Russia."

"You sound German to me," Mrs. O'Reilly says.

I bob my head. "Yes. German," I say.

She sighs. "I married a German once," she tells me in German.

I smile at her. Married a German! And she knows the language, too!

But my smile falls when she adds, "I was young and foolish then."

"Oh," I say.

"Come in anyway," she says.

I step into the foyer. A gleaming staircase winds to the upper floor. Overhead, a chandelier shimmers. I've never been in a house so grand. How will I ever clean such a place?

"My German isn't good," she says.

"Neither is my English," I tell her.

"We will have to make do," she says, sighing again.

I spend the next few hours sweeping and mopping the floors, which were barely even dirty, and polishing the silverware and mirrors. Mrs. O'Reilly watches me the entire time, saying nothing while following me with crossed arms. When I finish the floors, she kneels down and examines them. When I finish polishing the silverware, she takes each piece out and holds it to the light.

In late afternoon, Mrs. O'Reilly stops me. My shoulders ache, and I hope she will tell me she wants to hire me and that it's time to go home. But instead, she says, "Now I'd like to test your cooking skills," she says.

I swallow hard. I forgot about the cooking part. I know how to cook. In Russia, Katarina and I took turns cooking for the family. But I only know German and Russian dishes. Surely she doesn't want *knoephle* (dumpling) soup or *krautsalat* (cabbage salad)!

Mrs. O'Reilly seems to read my mind. "Make me your favorite dish," she says, leading me into the pantry. "It doesn't matter what it is."

I find everything I need to make the dumpling soup — dough, potatoes, and ham. I set the table for one, but Mrs. O'Reilly insists I sit down to eat with her. When she tries my soup, I study her face. I can't tell if she likes it or not. When she is finished, she pushes back her bowl. "I liked it," she says. "It reminds me of home."

I am so relieved I almost fall off my chair. I don't know what she means by home, but I don't ask.

"You must be tired," she says. "Go home now, but come back tomorrow. I will make my decision by the end of the week."

———✕———

For the rest of the week, I do every single thing Mrs. O'Reilly asks. And more. She stops following me around and instead lets me clean on my own. Every night before I leave, she checks my pockets to make sure I haven't stolen anything.

On Saturday she hands me an envelope. "Here is your pay," she says. "Come back Monday."

Finally, something has gone right in America.

———✧———

Mr. Schweitzer smiles when I tell everyone I've been hired by Mrs. O'Reilly. But Katarina and Mrs. Schweitzer don't look happy. Katarina shoots jealous glances at me. "I wish we could switch places one day," she mutters. "Then you'll know what it means to work."

Mrs. Schweitzer says nothing to me, but I know she is disappointed. The more money I make, the sooner we will leave.

For the next two weeks, I work as hard as I can for Mrs. O'Reilly. I clean her cupboards and her pantry. I wash her bedding and her clothes. I climb onto a ladder to clean her high windows and light fixtures.

I don't know what to think about Mrs. O'Reilly. She is stern and wary of me, but she isn't unkind. And she likes my cooking.

I make her lunch, and she makes me sit and eat with her at the long, gleaming oak table. We eat mostly in silence, sometimes exchanging a few words in German. After a few days, Mrs. O'Reilly says, "From now on, we will not speak German in this house."

I cast my worried eyes downward. When I look back up, she gives me a tight smile. "You need to learn English," she says. "And I will help you."

Chapter 15
Mrs. O'Reilly's Story

Each day I go to Mrs. O'Reilly's. In the mornings, I sweep, dust, do the laundry, and cook. In the afternoons, Mrs. O'Reilly asks me to sit with her on her wide front porch and talk in English. She reads newspaper articles aloud and asks me to explain what they say. She points to various objects — trees, birds, bicycles, clouds, windows, shoes — and tells me the English names. At first, speaking aloud in English makes me nervous, but as the days go on, I grow more comfortable with my pronunciations.

One day, she looks me square in the eye and says,

"You are a smart girl. You should be in school, not working for me."

I shrug. "I need money. To join Father."

"Did you think this is what America would be like?" she asks.

I don't know the English words to explain how I feel. "No," I say. I want to ask her a question, and I think carefully how to phrase it. "Why are you helping me?"

Mrs. O'Reilly is silent for a moment. She stares into the distance, then turns to me. Her eyes sparkle with tears.

"I was once like you," she tells me. "I was an immigrant, too."

I am stunned. "You? But . . ." I look around at her big house, her jeweled fingers, her expensive clothing. How could she ever have been like me?

"I came from County Clare, Ireland," she tells me. "I wasn't much older than you. And I was all alone. I had nothing but a suitcase."

Life in Ireland was hard, she tells me. She was born during the Potato Famine in the 1840s. When disease caused potato crops to fail, hunger broke out across Ireland.

"We were destitute," she tells me. "We lived as beggars on the streets. My mother fell ill and died. My father wanted me to have a better life, so he saved every penny he could to send me to America. The day I boarded the ship was the last time I saw him."

I think about Ruth, who also crossed the ocean alone. But at least she had a father waiting for her.

"You didn't know anyone here?" I ask.

Mrs. O'Reilly shakes her head. "In those days, many Irish women came to this country alone. Some found jobs as servants, like you, or in garment factories, like your sister. Others worked in textile mills or became Catholic nuns. We found ways of supporting ourselves, without having husbands to rely on."

I can't imagine elegant Mrs. O'Reilly ever working in a factory. "What did you do?" I ask.

"First, I worked in a textile mill in New England. The conditions were horrible. I worked long hours. I slept in a boardinghouse, crammed together with other working girls. And rats. Lots of rats!" She laughs. "After two years, I was still making the same wages and living in the same awful conditions. So I decided to use the little money I'd saved to come to Chicago. Conditions here weren't much better, and I worked in a factory for several more years. I lived in the cheapest, worst boardinghouse I could find."

"Why?"

"I wanted to save every penny to pursue my real dream." Mrs. O'Reilly pauses and smiles at me, waiting for me to ask.

"What was your dream?"

"To become a banker."

A banker! I've never heard of a female banker before.

Mrs. O'Reilly laughs at my shocked expression. It's the first time I've ever heard her laugh.

"I started by lending money to poor immigrant women, to help them better themselves" she explains. "When they paid me back, I invested the money. Slowly my business grew. I rented an office downtown and hired immigrant women to work for me. Eventually I made enough money to pursue my other dream."

"What was that?"

"To open my own dress shop. Gowns by Kathleen." She smiles proudly. "The store did so well that I opened another one in New York. Then in Paris and then London!"

I am surprised again. A banker and a dress designer! "And then you met your husband?" I ask.

She glances at me, puzzled. "Oh, him!" she says finally. "Yes, my German husband. We had a son together. But he didn't like my independent ways. Thought I should be a more traditional wife. He left, and I never saw him again. I've been single ever since."

I am confused. "You are Mrs. O'Reilly. So who was Mr. O'Reilly, then?"

"That's my maiden name. I went back to it after my husband left us."

I sit silently, taking in her story. I never imagined a woman, a poor immigrant woman at that, being able to make money on her own, without a husband. And not just a little money, but a lot. Enough to own a house like this one!

"Now you know my story," Mrs. O'Reilly says. "What do you think?"

I smile at her. "America is better than I ever dreamed!" I say.

Chapter 16
The Letter

That night, I lie awake, turning Mrs. O'Reilly's story over in my head. I always imagined I would become a wife and mother someday. Like my own mother and grandmother. It's what women have always done in our culture. But now, here in America, I have other options. I could become a businesswoman like Mrs. O'Reilly. Or maybe I could even do both — have a career and a family. Here in America, anything seems possible.

I wish I could talk to Ruth. I know she would love to hear Mrs. O'Reilly's story.

A few days later, a letter from my father arrives. Inside the envelope is another letter, addressed to me. Ruth! I tear the letter open. But the words are not in Russian. The letter is in English. And I can't read it. I recognize a word here and a word there, but not enough to understand what Ruth is telling me.

Frustrated, I fold the letter and stuff it in my pocket. I look up to see Katarina watching me. "What was that?" she asks. "From your Jewish friend?"

I nod and look away.

"Ruth?" Helene pipes up. "I really liked her!"

"Me too," I say.

Katarina reads Father's letter aloud. Halfway through, Helene bursts into tears. Karl's lip trembles, too. "What is it?" I ask, drawing them both close.

"I miss Father!" Helene says, her voice muffled in my sleeve. "When will we get to go live on the farm with him?"

I glance at Katarina, and she looks back at me with weary eyes. "Soon," I say.

Even though I know Mrs. O'Reilly's immigrant story, I still feel a little shy around her. The next day, as we are sitting on her porch, she pulls out the newspaper. "What should I read today?" she wonders aloud.

"I have something," I tell her. I take Ruth's letter and hand it to her. "This is from a friend I met on the journey to America. I can't read it."

Mrs. O'Reilly takes the letter and looks me over. "You can't read?"

"Yes," I say quickly. "I can read German and Russian. But she wrote in English."

She nods. "I'll read it to you," she says.

Dear Emma,

I am writing to you in English because I need to practice. You know English now, right? I hope so, otherwise you won't be able to read this!

You will not believe what happened on Ellis Island! My

father got the date wrong, so he was not there when I arrived. I was so scared! I didn't know what had happened to my father. Was he dead? Had he forgotten about me? I couldn't imagine having to go back to Russia alone.

The immigration officials wouldn't let me off the island until my father came. I kept staring at the Statue of Liberty, thinking I could swim across to her. She would welcome me, right? I know it sounds silly, but that's what I was thinking.

When my father didn't come, the officials sent me to another building, where there was a big room with lots of beds. They told me they would send a telegram to my father. If he didn't come, I'd have to go back to Russia. I couldn't sleep that night. I don't think anyone slept. All night I heard people tossing and turning and sobbing. We were all scared of being sent away.

The next morning I went to the rooftop with some other children. On the rooftop was a playground, with two slides and some swings. I played with the little children. If they fell and got hurt, I wiped away their tears. I kept hoping the immigration officials would see how helpful I was and let me through to America.

From the rooftop we could see the buildings of New York. I knew my father was there, somewhere, in those tall buildings. If only he would come for me!

At last I heard my name being called. My father was here! I couldn't even see where I was going because my eyes were filled with tears. I almost didn't recognize my father because it had been so long since I'd seen him.

I was so happy to leave the island, but I felt terrible for all the other children who might be sent back. I still think about them sometimes and hope they are okay.

I think about you a lot, too. Do you like America? I do. But it's not what I imagined! After my father picked me up from Ellis Island, we went to the apartment where he lives with my aunt and cousins. The apartment is on the Lower East Side in New York. It is very small. Father says someday we might get our own apartment. I can't wait for that day! I sleep in the kitchen with my cousins, and it's very cramped and hot.

Almost everyone in our neighborhood is Jewish. Sometimes it doesn't feel any different than life in Odessa. Father works all the time at a store down the street, and I go to school. At first I was very lonely, but I've made some new friends.

My older cousin Rachel works at a shirtwaist factory. When I get old enough, I want to work there, too. But she says the work is hard, and she doesn't get paid much.

I am glad to escape the Jewish pogroms in Russia. Sometimes, I still get called names, but mostly people leave us alone. I'm glad we don't have to be afraid anymore.

Please write soon. I want to hear about your life on the farm.

Love,

Ruth

After she finishes reading, Mrs. O'Reilly hands the letter back to me. "Wait here," she says and goes into the house.

I can't wait to write back to Ruth and tell her about everything that has happened to me. I will have to use my wages to buy pen and paper, because I know the Schweitzers don't have any to spare.

My mind is racing so fast that I barely notice when

Mrs. O'Reilly comes back out and sets down a pen and paper in front of me. I begin to write Ruth's name, but Mrs. O'Reilly stops me. "You will write Ruth back," she tells me. "But in English. You can speak well now, but you need to learn to read and write, too." She smiles. "And I will help you."

Chapter 17
Dear Ruth

Dear Ruth,

I am sorry it has taken me so long to write back. But Mrs. O'Reilly said I needed to write you in English, and it took some time to learn. You are probably wondering who Mrs. O'Reilly is. I have so much to tell you!

At Ellis Island, we thought we'd be sent back because my brother Karl had a twitch in his eye. But he was cleared, and we boarded a train for Chicago. When we got to Chicago, we found out my older brother, Gustav, had lost all our money. Long story! We didn't have enough for tickets to

North Dakota. So I sold my earrings (you remember my gold earrings?) to a man on the street. But it was only enough for two tickets. Father and Gustav went, and the rest of us stayed with the Schweitzers in Chicago. They made us pay to live with them.

Katarina got a job at a garment factory, and I cleaned house for an Irish woman, Mrs. O'Reilly. She taught me to speak English. After I got your letter, she insisted I learn to read and write in English, too.

We finally saved up enough money for tickets to North Dakota. The train ride was long. I can't believe how big this country is! My father met us at the train station and took us to our new home on my uncle's farm.

At first I was scared. So much wide-open space! You can see for miles, and there's not another house in sight. Just fields and more fields, all the way to the horizon. It is so different from Odessa and Chicago, where people are piled on top of each other. And it is very quiet. At night, you can hear every chirping cricket. Sometimes the wind blows so hard I think the house will topple over!

Now that I am used to living in the country, I love it. In the mornings, before the sun is even up, Katarina and I milk the cows. Katarina is not as bossy and grumpy as she used to be. It seems like we've both grown up so much since coming to America.

After we milk the cows, we go to school on an old horse named Nell. Katarina and I both fit on her back. She doesn't go very fast, but Father says that's good, because then we won't get as hurt if we fall off. The school is miles away, and it's not in a town. It's a country school, one big room. We have one teacher for all the grades.

When my father sold his wheat after the fall harvest, he gave us each a bit of money. Gustav went to town, and I was scared he was going to lose all his money again. But when he came back, he held out his hand to me. In his palm was a pair of gold earrings!

I have to save enough paper to write to Mrs. O'Reilly, so I will stop for now. It is funny to think about how different my life is than yours. But we are really not so different after all, are we?

Love,

Emma

A NOTE FROM THE AUTHOR

My great-grandmother Emma (right) and her sister Clara

In 1909, when she was seventeen years old, my great-grandmother, Emma Weisz Reiser, left her home in Russia (present-day Ukraine) for a new life in America.

I always knew my great-grandmother had emigrated from Russia. As a child, I was interested in history and family, and I longed to know more.

"Ach," my great-grandmother would say in her thick accent. "That's all in the past. A long time ago." And it was a long time ago. My great-grandmother lived to be nearly 102 years old.

At age 96, she broke her hip and moved in with her daughter, my maternal grandmother, Eleanora. When I was a teenager, I helped take care of her on some afternoons. While we sat together, she would sometimes just gaze out the window. I would look into her blue eyes and wonder what she was thinking. Was she remembering being a girl in Russia? Was she remembering crossing the ocean to a strange land? I thought about everything those blue eyes had seen — the invention of automobiles, airplanes, television, and computers — and how much the world had changed in her lifetime.

Over the years, I have loved to listen to my grandma Eleanora tell about her mother's immigrant experience. Although *Emma's New Beginning* is a fictional story, I used some details from my great-grandmother's life. Like the Emma of the book, my great-grandmother Emma grew up near Odessa in a German community. She could speak both German and Russian, and she attended a Russian school.

To avoid being forced to serve in the Russian army,

Emma's older brothers, Peter and Albert, decided to immigrate to America. The brothers, who were young men in their early twenties, saved money for their trip. Unfortunately, they lost the money in a card game. To help pay for more tickets, Emma's father sold her gold earrings. The boys were then able to go to America.

In May, 1909, my great-grandmother Emma, along with her parents, Rosina and Gustav, and her younger siblings Odelia, Jacobina (Clara), Robert, Christian, and Louise, boarded an enormous ship, *The Virginian*, bound for America. They had to stay below deck in steerage, along with other immigrant families. Giant waves tossed the ship about, and Emma got terribly seasick. Later, when she spoke about the crossing, she said she never wanted to travel by ship again. And, most of all, she remembered being scared.

In June, the ship reached Ellis Island. During the immigration process, health inspectors discovered a problem with twelve-year-old Robert's eyes. "He was just cross-eyed," my grandma Eleanora explained. But even so, the family was detained. Unlike Karl in the book, who was allowed to continue, Robert was quarantined for three weeks. My great-grandmother and her family stayed on the island, waiting until Robert was released.

The family then went to Canada and boarded a train bound for Winnipeg, Manitoba. They stayed in Canada for about a year, and Emma served as a companion to a Jewish woman. When Emma left to go to North Dakota, the woman cried to see her go. They knew they'd never see each other again.

Emma's family settled on a farm near Underwood, North Dakota. There, my great-grandmother met and married Gottfried Reiser, a German whose parents had also emigrated from Russia.

When I was preparing to write the book, I asked my grandma Eleanora once again to tell me about her mother's experience. She told me everything she knew

My great-grandmother Emma on
her wedding day.

about Emma's trip across the ocean and her new life in America. And then she smiled and said, "And now here we are!"

"Yes," I agreed. "Here we are."

JESSICA GUNDERSON grew up in the small town of Washburn, North Dakota. She has a bachelor's degree from the University of North Dakota and an MFA in creative writing from Minnesota State University, Mankato. She has written more than fifty books for young readers. Her book *Ropes of Revolution* won the 2008 Moonbeam Award for best graphic novel. She currently lives in Madison, Wisconsin, with her husband and cat.

MAKING
CONNECTIONS

1. In your own words, summarize why Emma's dad decided the family should leave Russia and move to America.

2. Why do you think the author chose to include two letters near the end of the story? What effect does this have?

3. Emma sold her earrings so that she could buy two train tickets. What does this tell you about Emma's character?

4. What are some of the different ways America gets described throughout the novel? Find specific words that characters use to describe it.

5. Compare Ruth and Emma using examples from the text. How are the girls different? How are they the same?

6. How would you describe the setting of the novel? Does the setting change?

GLOSSARY

boardinghouse (BOR-ding-houss)—a place where people pay to live and receive daily meals

customs (KUHSS-tumz)—actions or ways of behaving that are common to a place or to a group of people

czar (ZAR)—also spelled tsar, the ruler of Russia before the revolution of 1917

destitute (DESS-tuh-toot)—very poor and unable to buy food, clothes, and shelter

detained (di-TAYND)—to keep a person from leaving

examination (eg-zam-uh-NAY-shuhn)—a careful check by a doctor to see if a person is sick or injured

ferry (FER-ee)—a boat or ship that regularly takes people across a certain stretch of water

immigrant (IM-uh-gruhnt)—someone who moves to another country, usually to live in the new country permanently

infirmary (in-FUR-mur-ee)—a place where sick people are treated and cared for

interpreter (in-TUR-pri-tur)—someone who can speak multiple languages and translates for others

lurch (LURCH)—to move in an unsteady and jerky way

pogrom (puh-GRUHM)—mob attacks on minority groups, especially Jews, that are allowed by the government

steerage (STEER-ij)—the part of a ship for passengers who bought the cheapest tickets

strike (STRIKE)—a period of time when workers refuse to work until their employer gives them better pay and/or better working conditions

trachoma (truh-KOH-muh)—a serious eye disease that spreads very easily and if untreated can cause blindness

Read more about the
people and events behind U.S. Immigration
in the 1900s with

CONNECT

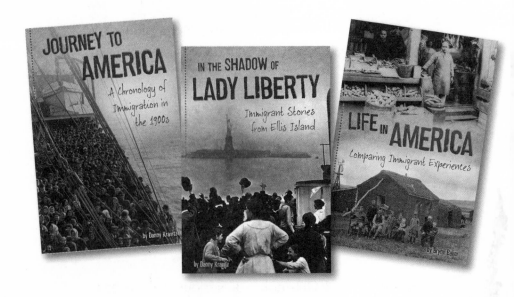

Or discover great websites and books like this
one at **www.facthound.com.** Just type in the
book **ID: 9781496505002** and you're ready to go.